SUPER PUZZLES AND FUN

by the Editors of Chickadee Magazine

**Written and Illustrated
by Debi Perna**

Owl
Owl Books

Owl Books are published by Greey de Pencier Books Inc., 179 John Street, Suite 500, Toronto, Ontario M5T 3G5

Debi Perna is a Contributing Editor of *Chickadee* Magazine.

"Puzzles and Fun" appears in each issue of *Chickadee*, a discovery-oriented magazine for kids aged 3 to 9. For more information, or to subscribe, send a letter with your name and address to *Chickadee*, 179 John Street, Suite 500, Toronto, Ontario, Canada M5T 3G5. In the United States, contact *Chickadee*, 25 Boxwood Lane, Buffalo NY 14227-2780.

Chickadee, OWL and the Owl colophon are trademarks of Owl Communications. Greey de Pencier Books Inc. is a licensed user of trademarks of Owl Communications.

Distributed in the United States by Firefly Books (U.S.) Inc., 230 Fifth Avenue, Suite 1607, New York, NY 10001.

This book was published with the generous support of the Canada Council, the Ontario Arts Council, and the Government of Ontario through the Ontario Publishing Centre.

Canadian Cataloguing in Publication Data

Perna, Debi.
        Super puzzles and fun from Chickadee Magazine

ISBN 1-895688-25-6

1. Puzzles – Juvenile literature. I. Title.

GV1493.P47 1995   j793.73   C94-932078-1

Designed by Word & Image Design Studio

Also available:
The Chickadee Book of Puzzles and Fun

Printed in Hong Kong

A   B   C   D   E   F

Super Puzzles and Fun

Here's a surprise just for you from *Chickadee* Magazine: a whole book of puzzles and fun, jokes and poems. Inside you'll help a cat find its friend, visit a farm, learn a mysterious musical code and lots more. You'll count, match, join the dots and learn new games to play, indoors and out.

Look at the top corner of every page to find an extra treat! These special little pictures make up a flip book. Flip through the pages, running the top corner quickly past your thumb, to make the picture seem to come alive! There's one moving picture as you flip from the front of the book to the back, and another as you flip from the back to the front.

Now let's discover some special times and places. Just grab a pencil and let the chickadees show you the way!

Cozy Cat Maze

Can you help this cat find its friend?
Trace a path from start to finish.

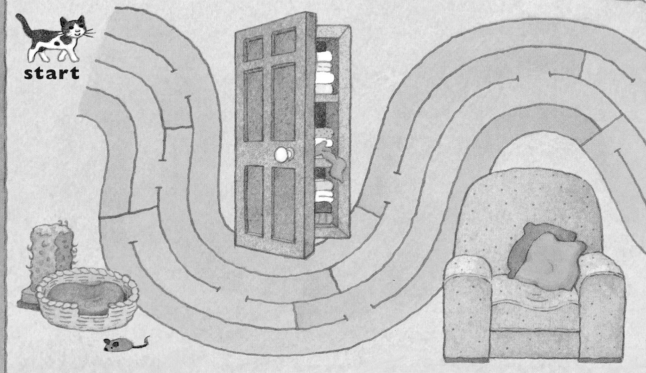

start

A mouse is in the house

Can you spot five soft places where a cat would like to curl up?

Whisper Game

Whisper a short message to a friend. Then your friend whispers what he heard from you to another friend. Keep the message going until everyone has passed the message along. The last person tells everyone what she heard. Is it the same as your message?

I like to ice skate or play in the snow.

Answer: A cat would be comfortable in the cat bed, in the closet on the towels, on the easy chair, on the rug in front of the fire, and in the open drawer.

finish

Did you know that no two cat nose prints are alike?

I like to ice cake with plain snow.

Where did the farmer take his pigs on a sunny Sunday afternoon?

On a pig-nic!

Morning Match Up

Draw lines to match each baby to its home, breakfast, and parent.

Babies

Homes

a. b. c. d.

Breakfasts

a. b. c. d.

Parents

a. b. c. d.

What do mice wear to the gym?

Squeakers

I made the first match.

Answer: bunny, b, d; baby, a, c, a; colt, d, a, c; duckling, c, d, b.

Family Pictures

Fill in the blanks with the missing letters to see
which family pictures are on this fridge.

Why should you bring your uncles to your family picnic?

To keep the ants company!

This word is "dad"!

Ready for school?

Going to School

Can you trace a path through the maze from each home to the school?

Why do mother kangaroos hate rainy days?

Because their children have to play inside.

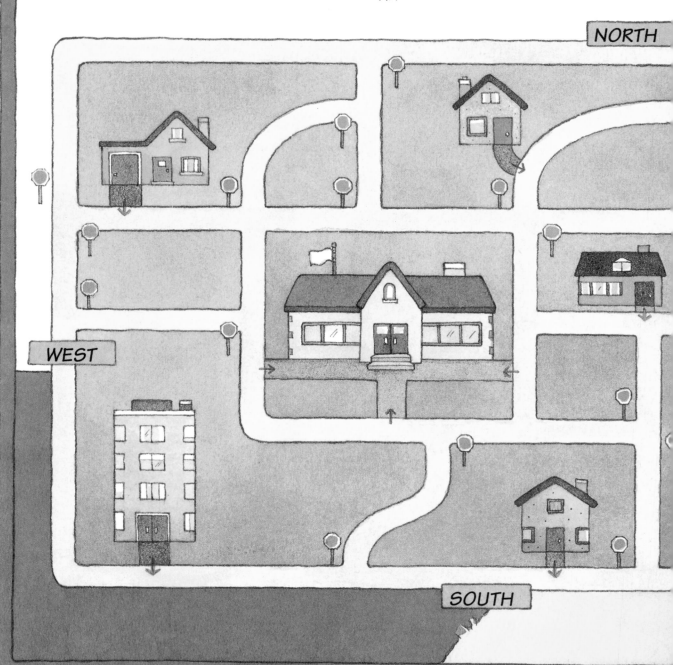

NORTH

WEST

SOUTH

8

Answer: There are 21 stop signs.

Red Light, Green Light

Have you played this game? One player, the caller, stands facing a wall or tree. The other players stand on an imaginary line about 20 giant steps behind her. The caller shouts "green light" and everyone races towards her.

When she calls "red light" everyone freezes. Then the caller turns around quickly to see if she can catch anyone moving. Anyone caught moving has to go back to the beginning. The first player to reach the caller is the caller next time.

How many stop signs can you count?

EAST

More signs on the next page!

Pick the Pairs

Each of these things has an opposite.
Draw lines to match them up.

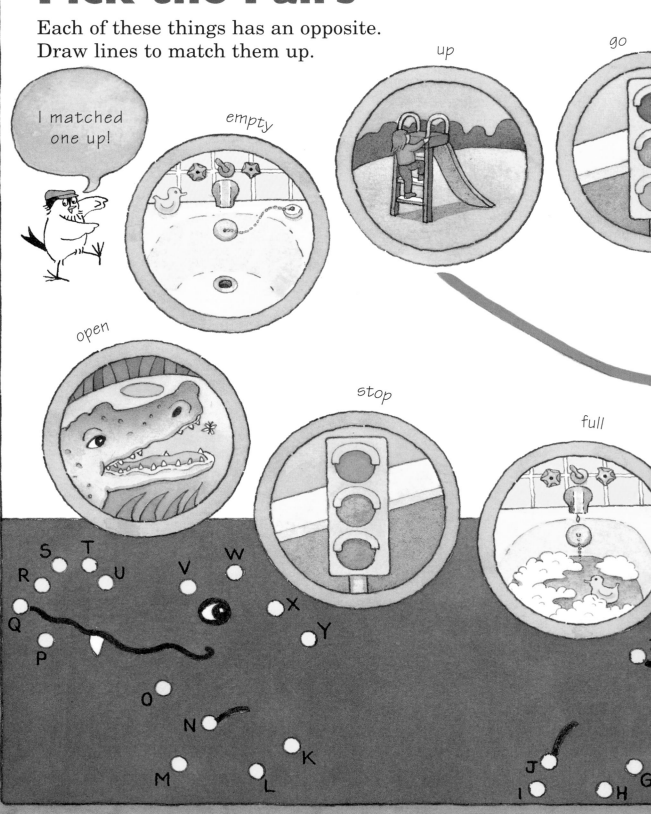

I matched one up!

empty

up

go

open

stop

full

S T W V
R U
Q
P
O
N K
M L J I H G

Answer: empty and full, up and down, go and stop, closed and open.

Crossout

Cross out the signs that match.
Draw the last one in the box below.

I crossed out the two telephones.

closed

down

Dot to Dot

Join the letters to see who's hiding here.

Out on the Farm

Use lines to join up the cows that look alike.

These cows are the same type.

Cow Count

Start counting, and fill in the chart!

Holstein _____

Jersey _____

Hereford _____

Yikes!

Answer: 4 Holsteins, 3 Jerseys, 3 Herefords.

Old MacDonald's Puzzle

Fill in the blanks, and sing the song.

Rainy Rhyme

Eency Weency Spider climbed up the water spout.
Down came the rain and washed the spider out.
Out came the sun and dried up all the rain,
So Eency Weency Spider climbed up the spout again.

I did one for you.

Weather Words

Can you put these storm words in the crossword? Fill in the blanks.

thunder

lightning

rain

hail

blizzard

sleet

tornado

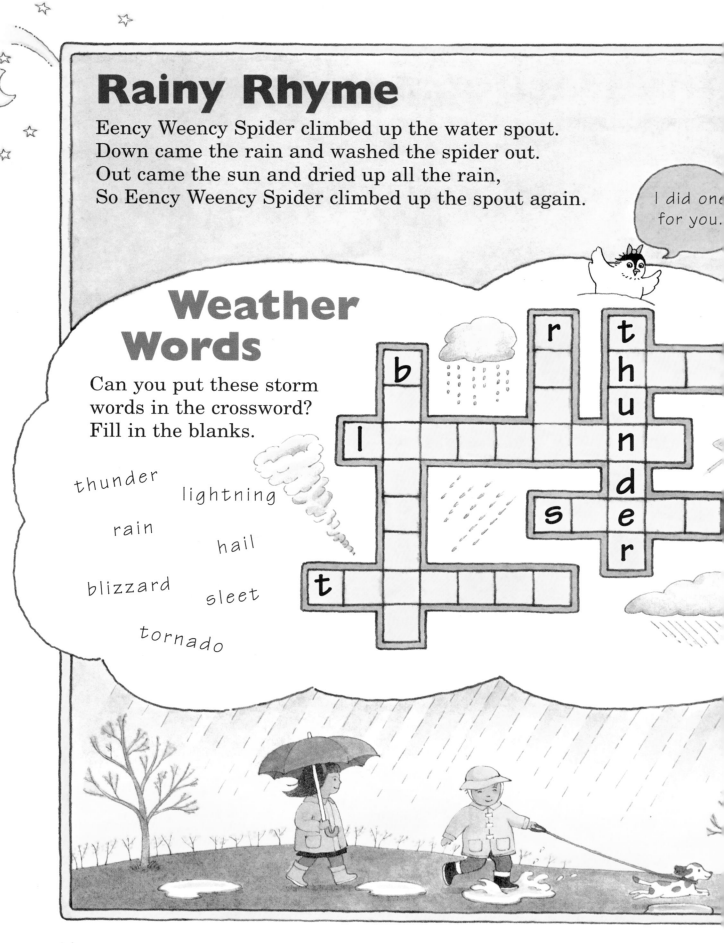

Window Watch

Draw a ✓ beside the things you see outside your window.

Name all the other things you see out your window.

15

Wet or Dry?

Match the wet things to the water. Match the dry things to the sand.

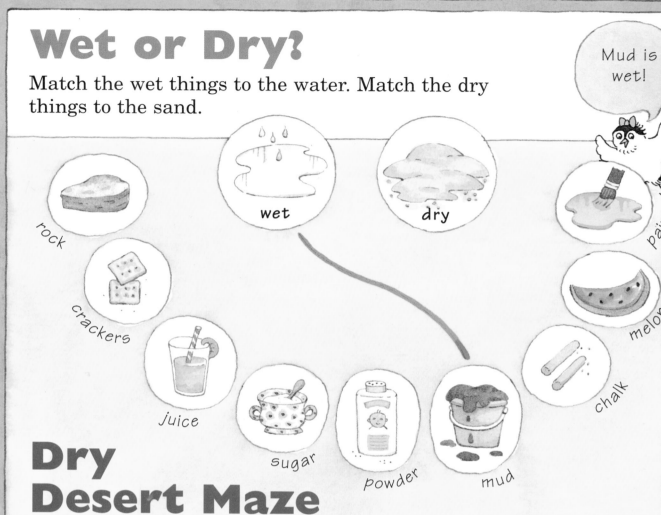

Dry Desert Maze

Can you get from start to finish through the cacti?

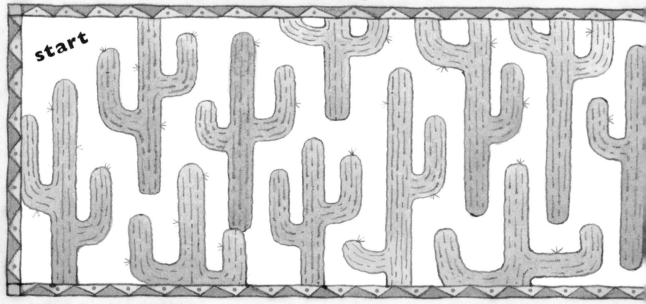

Answer: The juice, mud, melon, and paint are wet things. The rest are dry things.

Weather Watch

What's the weather like today where you live? Color the bar and trace one arrow to show your weather.

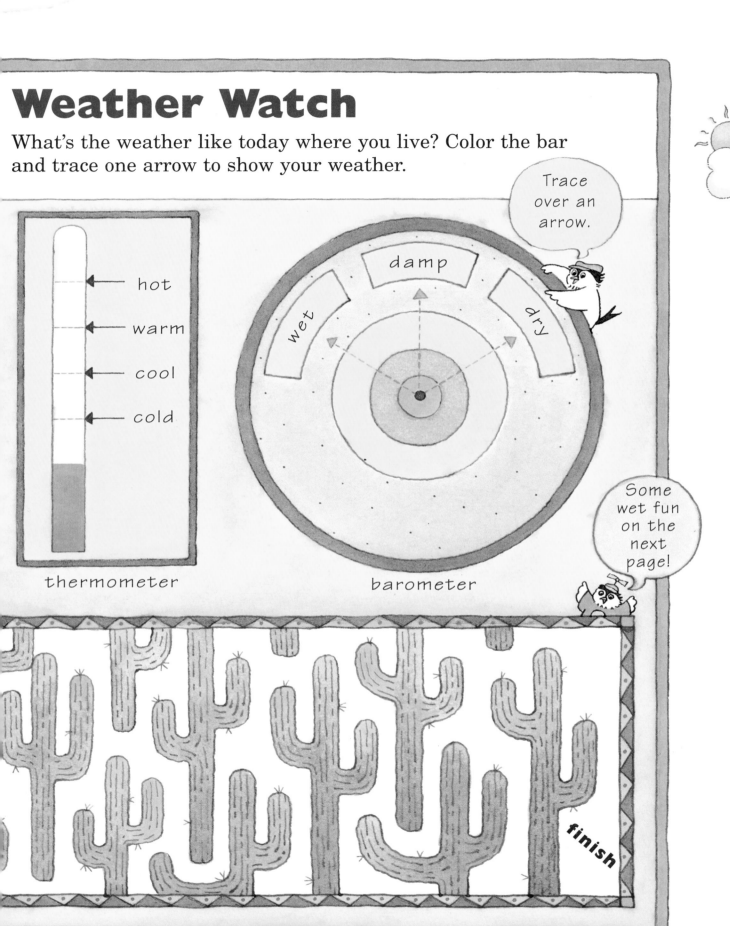

Trace over an arrow.

Some wet fun on the next page!

damp

wet

dry

hot

warm

cool

cold

thermometer

barometer

finish

Ticklefish

by Sylvia Morice

Ticklefish
Picklefish
Sell-them-for-a-nickel fish
Catch-them-in-a-paily fish
Trade-them-for-a-whaley fish
Faster-than-a-snaily fish
Fickle pickle
Ticklefish

Lots of Dots

Join the dots to see who's hiding in this pond.

Dragonflies live near ponds. How many can you spot here?

Sink or Float?

Draw a ⬆ beside the things that float.

Draw a ⬇ beside the things that sink.

A paddle floats.

paddle

water lily

rubber duck

penny

anchor

golf ball

life jacket

rock

beach ball

buoy

Fly or swim to the next page!

Answer: The paddle, water lily, rubber duck, life jacket, beach ball, and buoy all float. The rest sink.

19

How Many?

Count all the different kinds of birds and fish.
Fill in the chart below.

I did one for you already.
6
All Birds
All Fish

Answer: blackbirds, 6; robins, 8; geese, 4; All Birds, 18; sunfish, 10; walleye, 7; trout, 5; All Fish, 22.

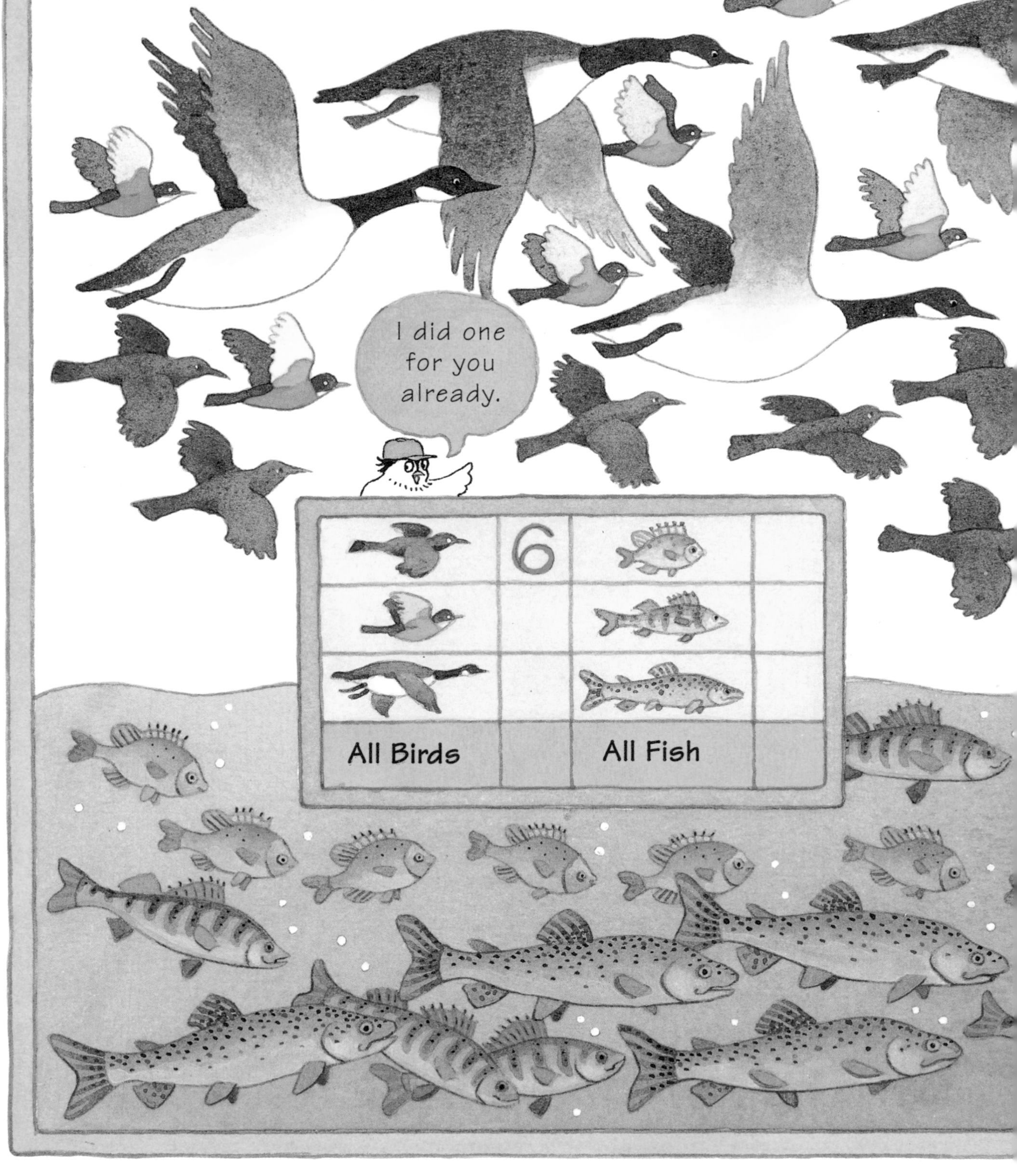

Group the Groups

Draw triangles to join up three things that belong in the same group.

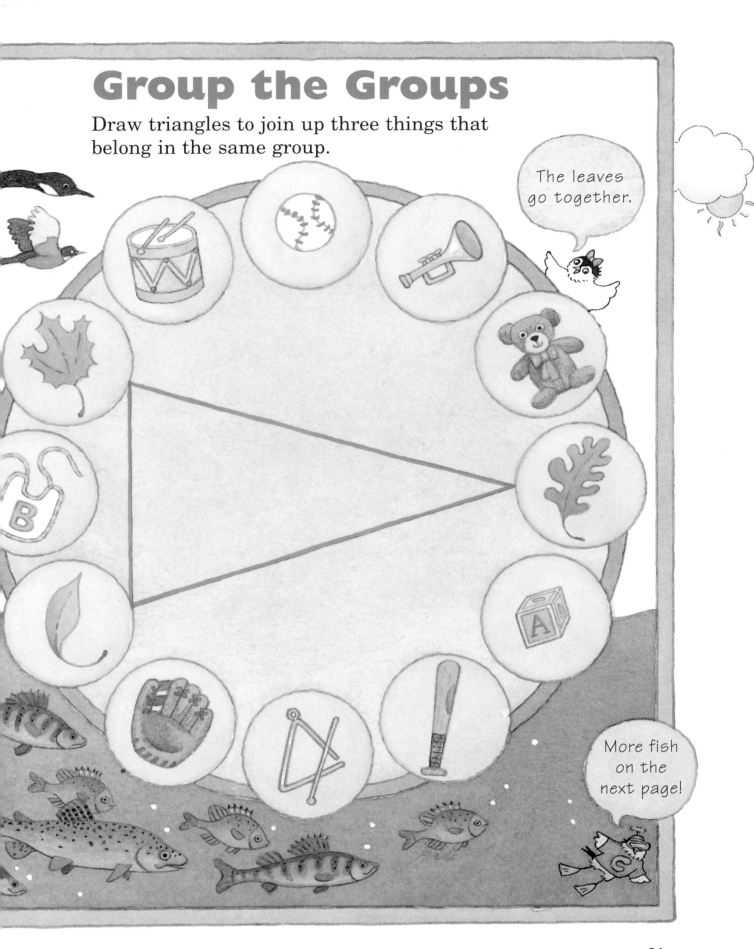

The leaves go together.

More fish on the next page!

Answer: three leaves; baseball, bat, and glove; teddy bear, block, and bib; triangle, drum, and horn.

21

Fishing at the Fair

Follow the lines to find out which fish each child has caught. Then match each fish number to a prize.

Quilt Count

How many of each patterned square can you count in the quilt? Fill in the blanks.

I filled in the first number.

6 ___ ___ ___ ___

Have fun at the fair!

Musical Maze

Can you solve the maze by finding the path that takes you past all the musicians?

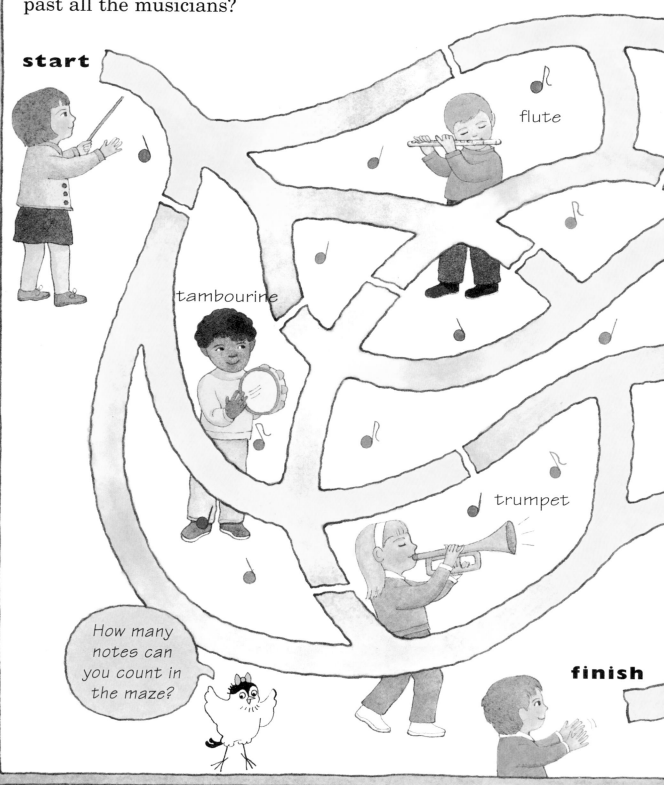

start

flute

tambourine

trumpet

finish

How many notes can you count in the maze?

Answer: 20 notes.

Music Note Code

Music notes are named with letters. Use the guide below to help you fill in the blanks and spell the hidden words.

Snowy Saturday

Which little pictures below are part of the big picture?

I think this picture belongs.

A.
B.
C.
D.
E.
F.
G.

How many things begin with "S" in this Saturday scene?

Answer: A, B, E, and F.
Answer: 10 "s" words; snow, six, shovel, sticks, scarf, smoke, sun, stripes, spots, stones. Did you find others?

What Comes Next?

Number the pictures in order from 1 to 6.

This picture comes first.

More fun comes next!

Grandma's Yarn

Which ball of wool is this grandma using? Which ball is the kitten playing with? Follow the yarn to find out.

Answer: grandma, A; kitten, B.

Knit Picks

Look at the knitted patterns in the shapes below. Then draw a ○, □, or △ around the clothes that have matching patterns.

The scarf matches the triangle pattern.

I counted two pairs of socks.

How Many?

sweater   scarf   mitts   hat   socks

Answer: square: c, e, h, k, l; circle: b, f, i, m; triangle: a, d, g, j, n.
Answer: sweaters: 3; scarves: 2; pairs of mitts: 4; hats: 3; pairs of socks: 2.

29

Day and Night

Draw a ☀ beside the words that have day in them.
Draw a 🌙 beside the words that have night in them.

daylight

daybreak

tonight

daylight

today

yesterday

Who's Hiding?

Can you name who's hiding here? Circle the
animals that come out at night.

One animal
looks like it
wearing a
mask!

a.

b.

c.

d.

e.

f.

g.

Answer: a, owl; b, raccoon; c, skunk; d, toad; e, cat; f, deer; g, rabbit. They all come out at night.

midnight

nighttime

midday

Midday has the word "day" in it.

daytime

daydream

nightie

nightmare

Eye Spy

How many pairs of eyes can you count shining in the dark?

People need more light to see at night. Starshine coming up!

Many animals have eyes that reflect light to help them see at night.

Nighttime Rhyme

To read this rhyme, follow the code and fill in the blanks.

☆ star   ☺ wish   🌙 tonight

☆ ____ light, ☆ ____ bright,

First ☆ ____ I see 🌙 _____,

I ☺ ____ I may, I ☺ ____ I might,

Have the ☺ ____ I ☺ ____

🌙 _____.

Good night!